School Stinks!

Paul Stewart is the very funny, very talented author of more than twenty books for children, including *The Edge Chronicles*, a collaboration with Chris Riddell.

Chris Riddell is a well-known illustrator and political cartoonist. His work appears in the *Observer* and the *New Statesman*, and he has illustrated many picture books and novels for young readers.

Both live in Brighton, where they created the Blobheads together.

All Blobheads titles can be ordered at your
local bookshop or are available by post from
Book Service by Post (tel: 01624 675137).

The Blobheads

School Stinks!

Paul Stewart
and Chris Riddell

MACMILLAN
CHILDREN'S BOOKS

P.S. For Joseph and Anna
C.R. For Jack

First published 2000 by Macmillan Children's Books
a division of Macmillan Publishers Limited
25 Eccleston Place, London SW1W 9NF
Basingstoke and Oxford
www.macmillan.co.uk

Associated companies throughout the world

ISBN 0 330 38974 2

1 3 5 7 9 8 6 4 2

A CIP catalogue record for this book is available from
the British Library.

Typeset by SX Composing DTP, Rayleigh, Essex
Printed and bound in Great Britain by Mackays of Chatham plc, Kent

Chapter One

"Six wives!" said Billy, as he collected his history project together. "Why couldn't Henry VIII just have one wife?"

He looked through the pages of writing and drawings.

"It made the homework so difficult!" he complained.

"Difficult?" said Derek, chewing thoughtfully on a felt-tip pen. "But surely six wives would make the homework easier. One to cook. One to wash-up. One to vacuum the carpets . . ."

"I said *home*work not *house*work," said Billy. "And that's the third pen you've eaten."

"But the ink is really delicious," said Derek. "Purple is my favourite."

Billy groaned. Blobheads! he thought. They travel halfway across the galaxy in search of the High Emperor of the Universe – and end up eating all my felt-tip pens.

"I'll tell mum and dad," he warned Derek.

"No!" said Derek, his blobby head pulsing with alarm. "Your parents must never find out about us."

"Then leave my pens alone!" said Billy.

"Sssh!" Zerek hissed from the cot in the corner of the room. "It has taken 47.6 minutes to get the High Emperor off to sleep. I do not want him woken again."

"He's *not* the High Emperor," said Billy. "He's my baby brother, Silas, and . . ."

"Lights out, Billy!" Mr Barnes called from downstairs. "School tomorrow."

"OK, Dad," said Billy, as quietly as he could.

"Is Silas asleep?" asked Mrs Barnes.

"Yes," replied Billy. "But not for much longer if you keep shouting like that," he muttered.

"N'night then, Billy," they both called.

"Goodnight!" Kevin the hamster shouted back.

"And don't you start!" said Billy. "It's bad enough that the Blobheads turned you into a talking hamster, without you rabbiting away all night."

"Well, pardon me for being nocturnal," Kevin said huffily. "And I don't *rabbit*!"

"He *hamsters*. Don't you, Kevin?" said Derek.

"Will you all be quiet!" Zerek hissed.

"All *right*!" said Billy.

He climbed into bed. The Blobheads stood in a cluster in their sleeping-corner and rested their blobby heads together. Billy switched off the light and was just falling asleep, when . . .

"Billy?"

Billy sighed. "Be quiet, Kevin."

"It wasn't me," the hamster squeaked indignantly.

The light went on. Derek was standing at Billy's desk. "It wasn't me, either," he said guiltily.

"It was me," said Kerek from the sleeping-corner. "Why *do* you go to school?"

"To learn things," said Billy. "All children go to school."

"Pfff," said Zerek. "We Blobheads know everything there is to know five minutes after leaving the egg."

"And anything we're not sure of, the Great Computer tells us," added Kerek.

Billy snorted. "The same Great Computer that brought you all the way to my bedroom and then left you stranded here, right?"

"The Great Computer works in mysterious ways," said Kerek mysteriously. "It knew the High Emperor needed protecting from the wicked Followers of Sandra . . ."

"Yeah, yeah," Billy yawned. "Derek, get back in your corner. And go to sleep, all of you."

He switched off the light. The room fell still.

"Billy?" It was Kerek again.

The light went on again. Billy sat up. "*Now* what?"

"You did say *all* children go to school?"

Billy rubbed his eyes. "Yes."

"Every single one?"

"Yes!"

"Even the High Emperor?"

Billy groaned. "One day, yes," he said. "Even Silas."

On hearing this, the three Blobheads let out a cry of alarm and huddled together. Their blobby heads flashed and fizzed.

"What?" said Billy. "*What?*"

Kerek looked up. "It is decided," he announced. "If the High Emperor is to attend this educational establishment then we must check it out at the earliest possible occasion."

"You mean . . ." Billy began.

"We will come to school with you to-morrow morning."

"Oh no, you won't," said Billy firmly.

"Oh yes, we will," the Blobheads chorused.

"Oh no . . ."

"OI! You lot!" came an angry voice. It was Kevin. "Keep the noise down. You're worse than a gaggle of squabbling gerbils – and you complain about *me* being noisy!"

"OK!" said Billy. "Keep your fur on!"

With the light off once and for all, Billy rolled over and tried to go to sleep.

He started counting sheep. But the sheep turned into queens, hundreds of them, each one with a golden crown perched on top of a curiously blobby head . . .

Asleep at last, Billy didn't notice the blobs on Kerek and Zerek's heads, still flashing and fizzing. Nor did he hear the faint rustle of paper.

"Yum," Derek purred and smacked his lips. "Deee-licious!"

Chapter Two

At a quarter past eight the following morning, Mr Barnes called upstairs. "Hurry up, Billy! Your breakfast's getting cold."

"I'll be right down," said Billy, then added, "What is it?"

"Something nutritious to set you up for the day," came his dad's cheery voice. "Kipper Kedgeree on a bed of garlic pineapple."

Billy groaned. "I suppose cornflakes are out of the question," he muttered.

"And why are you lot looking so pleased with yourselves?" he said, turning on the three grinning Blobheads.

"Nothing," said Kerek.

"Nothing at all," said Zerek.

"I told you last night," said Billy. "You are *not* coming to school. Is that clear?"

The Blobheads nodded.

"Christmas clear," said Derek.

Billy laughed. "It's *crystal* clear," he corrected him.

Derek frowned. "What is?" he said.

"Billy!" Mr Barnes shouted. "I won't tell you again. I . . . Alison," he said. "What's the matter?"

"My monthly sales report," came Mrs Barnes's anxious reply. "I can't find it anywhere. And I'm late enough as it is . . . It was on the sideboard. Billy? Have you seen my sales report?"

"No, Mum," he called back.

15

Behind him, Billy heard Derek burp.

"Derek!" said Billy. "You haven't had Mum's report, have you?"

"Report? What report?" said Derek innocently.

"It's full of graphs and figures and all bound up in a big blue and orange folder," Billy explained.

"No, I haven't," said Derek. "Though it sounds scrummy."

Billy pointed at the corner of the Blobhead's mouth. "Then what's that?"

Derek removed a fragment of paper with his tentacle and examined it.

"Well?" said Billy.

"It's . . ." Derek faltered.

"It's all right!" Mrs Barnes exclaimed. "I've found it! Billy, if you want that lift to school, you'll have to come now!"

"Coming!" Billy ran to the door. "Whoops!" he said, skidding to a halt.

16

"Nearly forgot my history project." He dashed back to the desk and gasped.

It wasn't there!

He stared at Derek. "What *is* that on your tentacle?"

Derek gulped guiltily. "A bit of King Henry, I think."

"You haven't . . . You couldn't . . ." Billy spluttered. "Are you telling me you've *eaten* my homework?"

"Derek!" said Kerek sternly.

"Typical!" stormed Zerek.

Derek looked round at the three angry faces, and turned a deep shade of purple. "It wasn't my fault," he wailed. "All those delicious colours . . . I just couldn't help myself."

"What am I going to do?" said Billy. "It took me all weekend. I can't go to school without it. Mr Trubshaw'll go mad!"

"Never fear," said Zerek calmly. "It's at times like these that we Blobheads turn to the Great Computer." He unclipped the small black box from the back of his belt. "Right. We simply tap in the information required. What was it? Henry the twelfth and his nine wives?"

"Henry the *eighth*," said Billy. "And he had *six* wives."

"Never fear," Zerek said airily, and pressed a button. "The Great Computer will sort out the details."

As Billy watched, the black box hummed and whirred, and sheet after sheet of paper emerged – each one covered in facts, figures and pictures. Zerek collected them up and slipped them inside a folder. Billy was amazed. It looked like an exact replica of the history project that Derek had eaten.

"There," said Zerek. "What could be simpler?"

"Billy!" shouted Mrs Barnes. "I'm going *now.*"

Billy snatched the folder, dashed downstairs, out of the front door and raced towards the car.

"Oh, for heaven's sake," said Mrs Barnes when he appeared. "Where's your hat, your scarf, your jacket? It's freezing!"

"I'll be all right," said Billy.

"Go and get them," said Mrs Barnes.

While his mum revved the engine impatiently, Billy raced back up the garden path, into the hall, grabbed his baseball cap, his Manchester United scarf and his padded jacket.

"Billy, your breakfast!" Mr Barnes called from the kitchen.

The cap burped quietly.

"Sorry, dad," said Billy. "No time."

"Another wonderful meal gone to waste," Mr Barnes complained. "I don't know why I bother. Slaving away over a hot stove . . ."

Beep! Beep!

"I'm *coming*!" Billy shouted.

As he climbed into the passenger seat, Mrs Barnes sped off.

"Sorry, love," she said. "But I can't afford to be late." She glanced round and frowned. "I don't remember seeing that hat before . . ."

Chapter Three

The bell had already rung when Mrs Barnes screeched to a halt in front of the school. Billy jumped out and trotted after the other late-comers.

"Nice hat, Billy," Gloria Wrigley giggled.

"Yeah, I didn't know it was fancy-dress today," Toyah Snipe tittered.

Billy did what he always did when Gloria and Toyah teased him. He ignored them.

It was only in the cloakroom when he

reached up to take his hat off that Billy discovered something was not quite right. It didn't *feel* like his baseball cap. He pulled it off. It didn't *look* like it either. Instead of the dark-blue cap with white stitching, he was holding a tall, purple top hat with red blobs.

"Waaaah!" he shouted.

"Waaaah!" yelled the hat, even louder.

"Kerek? Is that you?"

"Yes," came a voice. But not from the hat. It was the scarf talking.

"Zerek?"

"Present," said the jacket.

The hat chuckled. "It's me. Derek."

"You're all here," said Billy crossly. "And after everything I said!"

"We had to," said the scarf.

"Our mission is to ensure the well-being of the High Emperor," said the jacket.

"And I thought it might be a giggle," the hat added.

Billy shrugged. "It could be worse," he said. "At least you haven't turned into a giant fluffy blue kangaroo like you usually do, Derek."

"'Ere, Billy Barnes," came a voice. "What's going on?"

Billy turned to see Warren Endecott

standing in the doorway. He groaned. Of all the boys and girls at Juniper Street Juniors, Warren was the last person Billy wanted to meet. He was big. He was mean. No one messed with Warren Endecott.

"Pardon?" said Billy innocently.

"You were talking to your hat," said Warren.

Billy smiled nervously. "'Course I wasn't."

"You called it Derek," said Warren, moving closer. "Anyway, why are you wearing such a weird hat in the first place?"

"I . . . errm . . ." Billy was floundering. He looked at the blobby top hat. "It's my dad's. I was in a hurry. I put it on by mistake."

"By mistake?" said Warren. "*That!*"

Just then, Derek panicked. Suddenly,

instead of the blobby top hat, Billy found himself clutching a fluffy blue beret.

Warren's eyes nearly popped out of his head. "How did you do that?" he said.

"Do what?" Billy bluffed.

But Warren knew what he'd seen. He seized the beret. "Let's have a closer look," he said.

"NO!" Billy cried, and tried to snatch it back.

"Gerroff! said Warren gruffly and shoved him away. He inspected the beret, tugging, squeezing, prodding . . . "There must be a secret button or something. If I can just . . ."

"Waaaah!" squealed the beret. "That hurt!"

Warren jumped back. "What was *that*?" He turned on Billy. "Something odd's going on here," he said, his fists

clenching menacingly. "And you'd better tell me what it is. Or else!"

"I . . . errm . . . Ventriloquism," Billy said. "I've been learning how to throw my voice."

Warren pushed his face into Billy's. "Are you taking the mickey?" he said. "'Coz if you are, I'm going to pulp you, Billy Barnes. I'm going to pulverize you . . ."

"You don't understand," said Billy, weakly.

"Calling me thick, now, eh? Right, that's it . . ."

"Don't worry, Billy," came a small, yet determined voice. "Leave this to us."

As he heard the words, Billy also noticed a movement. The scarf round his neck was uncoiling and reaching down into the left-hand pocket of his jacket.

"The other side," the jacket hissed.

Warren's jaw dropped.

The end of the scarf reappeared. It was wrapped around what looked like a perfume bottle filled with purple liquid.

"What the . . .?" gasped Warren and Billy together.

"Hold your nose, Billy," shouted the scarf.

Billy did as he was told.

Warren had had enough. "You blooming weirdo!" he roared, and lunged forwards. "I'm gonna . . ."

"Now!" cried the jacket.

The scarf reared up, pushed the little bottle into Warren's face and removed the stopper. Warren's nose twitched. The stopper was popped back into place.

"D'ya know what, Billy Barnes?" said

Warren, his big fist resting on Billy's shoulder.

"Wh . . . what?" stammered Billy.

"You're the nicest boy in the whole school," he gushed, and a great gormless grin spread across his face. "Will you be my friend?"

"Your friend?" said Billy.

"Oh, please say you will."

"Just give me back my hat, Warren," said Billy.

Warren looked down at the beret. He held it out then, just as Billy was about to take it, snatched it back coyly. "Only if you promise me something."

"What?" asked Billy.

"Promise you'll play skipping with me at break-time."

"Skipping?"

"I *love* skipping," said Warren. "Oh, go on. Please."

"OK, then," Billy nodded. "I promise."

"Oh, thank you, Billy!" Warren cried. "Till break-time, then." And with that, he turned on his toes and tripped off to class.

The moment Warren was gone, Billy pulled off the scarf and the jacket and hung them on his hook with his hat. "You shouldn't have come here," he said angrily.

"Don't worry about us," said the jacket.

"I'm not!" said Billy. "I'm worried about everyone else in the school. What *have* you done to Warren?"

"Clever, eh?" said the beret, as it morphed into a pirate's tricorn hat. "It's called *Psychopong.*"

"*Psychopong?*" Billy shouted.

"Or *psycho-morpho-blobby-pong,*" to give it its full name," the jacket explained. "It's a mood modifier. We never go anywhere without it."

"It is useful when some of the more irrational species on Blob get out of hand," said the scarf. "But enough of this. You go to your lesson. We'll take a look round."

"Not with that stuff, you don't!" said Billy, snatching the bottle away from the scarf. He slipped it into his trouser pocket. "You've done more than enough already."

"Spoilsport," said the tricorn hat sulkily.

"Wait here till I get back," said Billy. "And I don't want to hear a peep out of you."

"A peep?" said the jacket. "Why would the most hyper-intelligent creatures in the universe wish to go *peep*? We can talk, you know."

"Well, don't!" Billy snapped. "Just stay silent. I'll come back at break-time."

The tricorn giggled. "You're playing skipping with Warren at break-time," it reminded him.

Billy groaned.

"It's OK," said the scarf. "The effects of *Psychopong* are strictly temporary. By break-time he'll probably want to beat you up instead."

Fighting or skipping with Warren Endecott? What a choice!

Billy wasn't sure which was worse.

Chapter Four

"Right," said Mr Trubshaw. "Your history projects. Did you all get them finished?"

"Yes, sir," came the hissing chorus.

"And I enjoyed every minute of it," Warren Endecott added, smiling sweetly.

"Quite," said Mr Trubshaw uncertainly. He looked round. "Who'd like to read out their work?"

"Me, sir! Me!" Warren cried eagerly.

Mr Trubshaw ignored him.

"Billy," he said. "How about you?"

Billy pulled the papers from his folder

and stepped up to the front of the classroom. He cleared his throat.

"Herbert the Eighth and his fourteen and a half wives lived in an extremely large house in . . ."

Billy stopped, aghast. *This* wasn't the homework he'd slaved over all weekend. His knees shook. His palms sweated. And, as a ripple of sniggering went round the room, his face turned bright red.

Voice quavering, he continued. "The number of wives proved very helpful when it came to housework. There was a wife for every chore. One for . . . the ironing." Billy swallowed. "One for . . ."

"Billy Barnes!" Mr Trubshaw bellowed. "What is the meaning of this? I've never heard such twaddle! This is . . . This is . . ."

Billy couldn't meet his teacher's stern gaze. He felt sick. He felt scared. The sniggering grew louder.

He knew he shouldn't. He knew it was foolish. But there was nothing else for it . . . Billy reached into his pocket. His fingers closed around the bottle.

"This is . . ." Mr Trubshaw roared for a third time.

Holding his breath, Billy whipped the *Psychopong* out, pushed it up to Mr Trubshaw's nose and removed the stopper for a second.

" . . . brilliant!" Mr Trubshaw exclaimed. "Inventive, imaginative – an absolute masterpiece."

The boys and girls of class 4T looked at one another in amazement.

"Never have I heard such a beautiful introduction to a history project." He wiped his eyes and sniffed. "I feel quite

overcome. I must . . . leave the room," he sobbed.

"Can we go and play skipping?" called Warren.

But Mr Trubshaw was gone. The sound of him trumpeting into his hand-kerchief echoed from the corridor. As Billy returned to his seat, everyone spoke at once.

"What did you do? What was that stuff?"

Gloria Wrigley tapped him on the shoulder. "Come on, Billy," she giggled. "You can tell me."

"No," said Billy.

"Oh, Billy," she wheedled. "Just . . ."

"Got it!" came a cry. While Gloria had kept him busy, Toyah had picked his pocket. She held up the bottle triumphantly.

"What is it?" said Gloria.

"Give it back!" shouted Billy.

"Perfume, I think," Toyah tittered. "Billy, you *shouldn't* have . . ."

She put it to her nose. Billy leapt forwards. "Don't!" he cried.

But it was too late.

Toyah removed the stopper and breathed in. The effect was instant. She turned on Billy and grabbed him by the lapels.

"Hey, dog-breath!" she bellowed.

"Fancy a knuckle-sandwich?" She drew her fist back threateningly.

"Oh, don't hit him!" Warren pleaded. "He's my best friend. We're playing skipping later."

"Put the stopper back in the bottle," said Billy, trying to remain calm. "Before things get out of control . . ."

But at that moment, Gloria made a grab for the bottle. Toyah spun round and threw a punch. As she did so, the bottle slipped from her grasp and crashed to the floor. The purple liquid spilled out and began to evaporate before their eyes.

At that moment, the door flew open and in flapped a jacket, a hat and a scarf. While the children stared, open-mouthed, the scarf jumped up, wound itself around Billy's neck and dragged him from the room, with the jacket and

hat close behind. The jacket slammed the door shut. The hat, now a gigantic red Santa bobble hat, bounced up and down.

"Red alert!" it squealed, and started to make a noise like a police siren.

"What the . . .?" said Billy.

"The situation is critical," the jacket shouted above the din.

"The door must be kept shut!" added

the scarf. "The effects will wear off eventually. I hope."

"You *hope*!" said Billy. "But . . ."

Kerek pointed at the window in the door. The classroom was full of purple mist.

"They've had too much," said Zerek.

"Far more than we'd give even the wildest boggle-beastie on Blob," said Kerek.

At the other end of the corridor, the headteacher's door burst open, and a short, portly woman in a tweed suit bustled out. It was Mrs Bleasdale. She looked confused.

"What is all that noise?" she yelled.

"Shut up, Derek!" Billy hissed.

The siren abruptly stopped. Mrs Bleasdale approached briskly.

"Ah, Billy," she said. "Whatever have you done to Mr Trubshaw? He's in my office in floods of tears over a magnificent piece of work you've done. I really must read it myself." She frowned. "But why aren't you in class? And where did you get that ridiculous hat?"

"I . . . errm . . ."

"Never mind that now," said Mrs Bleasdale. "Back inside with you. I'll be taking the rest of Mr Trubshaw's lesson."

Before Billy could warn her, the head-teacher seized the door handle and

marched into the classroom. The swirling purple mist poured out.

"Run, Billy!" came three insistent voices in unison.

Billy spun round. As he did so, the scarf, the jacket and the hat morphed back into Kerek, Zerek – and a giant fluffy blue kangaroo.

"Oh, Derek!" Billy exclaimed. "Not again!"

"Hold your nose!" said Kerek urgently. "And RUN!"

Billy, Kerek and Zerek dashed down to the bottom of the corridor, with the giant fluffy blue kangaroo bringing up the rear.

"This way," Billy yelled. He skidded round to the right and continued to the fire exit. The Blobheads went with him. Billy pushed the bar on the door, they all ran out and, *slam*!

"Phew!" said Kerek.

"Thank Blob," said Zerek.

"Where's Derek?" said Billy, looking round.

Zerek tutted. "Trust him!"

The three of them pressed their faces against the window and peered into the corridor. There was the giant fluffy blue kangaroo, wandering about with its paws clamped over its nose.

"Over here!" yelled Billy and hammered on the window.

At that moment, Mrs Pettifogg the school secretary appeared round the corner, eyes streaming and a handkerchief pressed to her nose, and ran straight into Derek.

"What the . . .?" she exclaimed. She seized Derek's fluffy blue ear in her vice-like grip. "You bust have got id

through the kitcheds. Those bloob-bigg didder ladies," she complained. "I'll have to call the authorities."

And with that, she dragged him back along the corridor.

"She can't!" Billy exclaimed.

"She already has," said Zerek glumly.

"But the *Psychopong*," said Billy. "Why hasn't it affected her?"

From inside came the sound of a muffled sneeze.

"With that awful cold?" said Kerek. "She can't smell a thing."

Chapter Five

The *Psychopong* had by now spread to every corner of the school. As Billy, Kerek and Zerek crept round the outside of the building, the scene through every window was one of utter chaos.

5P was bad. 6L was worse. Dancing. Shouting. Fighting.

"I'm a little flower!" came the gruff voice of the biggest boy.

"Do that again, Hermione, I'll break your legs," screamed a pale girl with blonde curls.

"Stop calling me names," said Mr Lander, "or I'll tell."

With a groan, Billy moved to the next window. Behind it was his own class. He gasped. If 5P was bad and 6L was worse, then 4T was as awful as it could possibly be.

Mrs Bleasdale was up on the front table – tweed skirt tucked into her pink knickers – conducting an aerobics class. "Jump and twist and *turn*!" she squealed enthusiastically.

Not that anyone was paying any attention. Gloria and Toyah were scrapping in the middle of the floor. Lucy Williams had Bruce Tully in a savage headlock.

"I want my mummy," he was howling.

The Taggart twins – the brainiest boys in the class – were being a train, chuffing happily up and down the aisles. Prim

Amelia Tilly was entertaining anyone who would listen with her musical burps. And Warren was racing frantically round the class with a skipping rope pleading for someone – *anyone* – to skip with him.

"You must stop this," Billy told the Blobheads.

"It won't be easy," said Kerek. "*Psychopong* is powerful stuff. As the *Book of Krud* warns us, 'Beware, for while a little *Psychopong* will modify the mangiest mood, too much will mangle the mind completely!'"

"But you've got to do something before the authorities arrive," said Billy desperately. "What about your Great Computer? I thought it could do anything."

From inside the classroom came a loud crash as Mrs Bleasdale lost her footing and plummeted to the floor. Luckily for the headteacher, her fall was broken. Unluckily for Warren, *he* broke it. The pair of them ended up sprawling on the floor, tangled up in the skipping rope.

"Will *you* play skipping with me?" Warren asked hopefully.

Billy turned on Kerek. "NOW!" he yelled.

Kerek removed the small black box from his belt and began stabbing at the buttons. The screen lit up and bleeped. He pressed some more buttons. Then some more . . .

"Well?" said Billy.

"There is something," said Kerek. "An antidote . . ."

Zerek squinted at the screen. "Of course," he said.

"What?" said Billy.

"*Psychopong* is a complex chemical compound," said Kerek. "To neutralize its effects we need an unbound emulsifying polymer."

"And have you got any?" said Billy.

The Blobhead shook his head.

"But what *is* it?" said Billy.

"It's sweet and yellow," said Kerek. "And milky thick."

"Derek had some for breakfast the other night," Zerek added.

For a moment, Billy looked confused. Then it dawned on him. "CUSTARD!" he shouted.

Holding their noses, Billy, Kerek and Zerek charged through the delivery door of the school kitchen. The dinner ladies didn't notice. They were all too engrossed in the rowdy football songs they were chanting.

"There's an Arsenal supporter in the storeroom!" Billy yelled.

With a cry of "let's get him!" the five women bundled inside. Zerek slammed the door and bolted it securely.

"Right," Billy announced. "You get started on the custard."

"And you?" said Zerek.

"I'm going to open every window in the school," he shouted as he rushed off. "And find out where Derek is."

While the school echoed and shook with the continuing madness, Kerek mixed 3.6 kilograms of custard powder with 1.8 kilograms of sugar and stirred it all into a thick paste with some milk. Meanwhile, Zerek filled an enormous pot with the rest of the 56 litres of milk, and brought it to the boil. Then, as Kerek poured one into the other, Zerek stirred vigorously with a wooden spoon. The thickening custard splattered everywhere.

"Mrs Pettifogg has got Derek locked in the stationery cupboard," said Billy, running back into the kitchen. "She's standing guard outside with a broom muttering something about giant rats, and that the authorities are on their way! We've got no time to lose . . ." He looked at the bubbling custard. "Are you sure this is going to work?"

Kerek dipped a tentacle into the custard and tasted it. "There's only one way to find out."

By the time they lugged the huge pot of custard to the serving-hatch, the Great Computer revealed that the *Psychopong* had finally cleared – even if its effects were continuing.

Billy stopped holding his nose and chalked up the day's menu on the blackboard. *Custard. Custard. Custard.* Then he grabbed the handbell and rang it at the dining-hall entrance.

From every part of the school, a cry went up and the corridors were suddenly jam-packed with famished pupils and teachers.

"Grub's up!" cried Mrs Bleasdale.

"Lunchy-poos!" shouted the Taggart twins.

"Oh, but I must think of my figure," said Warren.

"Out of my way!" roared Toyah.

"Stop pushing, or I'll tell," Mr Lander complained.

They burst into the dining-hall.

"CUSTARD!" everyone cried out on seeing the board, not stopping to look at the two blobby figures at the counter.

Dressed up in their dinner-lady outfits of green coats and white lacy caps, the two Blobheads could hardly keep up with the demand.

Billy slipped nervously in beside the Taggart twins and watched to see if the antidote would really work. There couldn't be much time left before the authorities arrived.

Gradually, one by one, eyelids began to droop, heads nodded, shoulders slumped. Warren's face plopped down

into his bowl of custard. The hall was silent but for the low rumble of gurgly snores.

"When they wake up again, everyone will be back to normal," said Kerek.

"I'll believe that when I see it," said Billy.

DDDRRRIIINNNGGG!

At the sound of the school bell, everyone's eyes snapped open.

"Billy Barnes!" came a voice. Billy looked round. It was Mr Trubshaw. "I haven't forgotten that atrocious piece of homework," he said. "I'll see you later."

"Yeah, me too," growled Warren Endecott, wiping custard from his ear.

"Kerek was right," Billy sighed. "Everyone *is* back to normal."

"'Ere we go! 'Ere we go! 'Ere we go!" came a chorus of raucous voices from the back of the kitchen.

"Who on earth is that?" asked Mrs Bleasdale.

"Neber bind that," said Mrs Pettifogg, striding into the dining-hall. "The authorities are here. I thig you'll want to see this, Headbistress."

"Me, too," said Billy, picking up the blobby coat and scarf on the counter, and following them out of the hall.

A moment later, Mrs Pettifogg, Mrs Bleasdale, Billy and Mr Smeal – a thin, balding man from the council with a net – were all standing in front of the locked door of the stationery cupboard.

"A bonstrous great rat," Mrs Pettifogg was saying. "Two betres tall, at least! But I banaged to pid it dowd."

"All right, madam," said Mr Smeal importantly. "Stand back. I'll deal with this."

He stepped forwards, net raised. He

turned the key in the lock. He turned the handle, pushed the door open and . . .

"Good grief! How on earth did that get in there?" said Billy, picking up a small blobby bobble hat from the floor.

Mr Smeal looked disappointed. Mrs Bleasdale turned to Mrs Pettifogg. "I must say, Muriel, your behaviour today has been most peculiar!"

*

Later that evening, Billy was finishing his re-written history project – Mr Trubshaw had insisted – when the Blobheads came bustling into the bedroom.

"School indeed!" Kerek was saying.

"The poor High Emperor," said Zerek. "I don't envy him."

"Oh, I don't know," said Derek. "I thought it was a giggle."

"So, what did you learn about?" asked Kevin the hamster.

Kerek and Zerek smiled. "Custard," they said.

"Custard?" said Derek. "Did I miss custard? Oh, I love custard. Though . . ."

Billy was collecting his papers together. Derek sidled over towards him and looked over his shoulders. "Mmm," he said and smacked his lips. "That looks nice."

"Derek!" roared Kerek and Zerek.

"You leave my homework alone!" shouted Billy.

"What?" said Derek, looking hurt. "Anyone would think I was going to *eat* it!"